Contending

For

Faith

A DOMESTIC VIOLENCE
A WARENESS STORY

Written by:

Latoya Jones-Frazier

ISBN-13: 978-0615609997

This book is dedicated to anyone who has been a victim of domestic violence, bullying and/or is suffering from any area of abuse.

TABLE OF CONTENTS

1
Waking Up On the Wrong Side of the Bed

I woke up and realized that I was on the floor. My head was throbbing, my lips were swollen, and the headache seemed worse than before. I should be used to this by now.

I made my way to the bathroom and looked in the mirror only to see myself as unrecognizable. I didn't recognize myself physically or mentally. I told myself that this is the last time I'll ever go through this again; I'd had enough.

I reached for an alcohol swab and dabbed my lip, oh how it hurt. As I stared at myself, I realized the need to save myself and get away from all the hurt and pain. The thing is, I had no one I can turn to and nowhere to go.

I decided at that moment, that it didn't matter where I went, any place I ended up, would be better than here.

I needed to clear my head and heal my body and soul. I planned on doing that by any means necessary.

I ran into the bedroom, and grabbed my Gucci bag. I began to pack it so fast you would think my name was Bo Jackson. However, "this" Bo didn't know everything. I didn't know what I was doing or what I had gotten myself into. I didn't know what my outcome would be.

However, I did know that if I didn't get away, the next time I fall, I might not get back up. I grabbed my personal belongings, and my wallet. Heck, I didn't care about anything else.

My goal was to get out of the house as quickly as I could, before he came home. I ran out of the bedroom, down the hallway, and as soon as I turned the corner...

Bang! His fist hits my face. I fell on the floor and clutched my bag. I thought that if I could just get past him, I might be able to make it outside. Justin begins to yell…

"Faith, where do you think you're going"? "Why do you want to keep pushing me? Don't you know that you make me do this", he shouts?

I say nothing. On the outside I'm bruised and on the inside I'm bruised. I'm what they call battered, mentally, physically and spiritually.

I call this love, however, there's something in my heart says, "what's love got to do with it"?

I sat on the floor crying, once again. I felt helpless and he's the one that's out of control. He starts ranting about all of the problems he's been having, especially out of me, but I haven't done anything wrong. I've just loved him unconditionally.

He bends down to hug me then he grabs my hands and kisses them.

He looks me in the eyes and says, "I'm sorry, I'm just not myself".

I began to cry even harder. I love him will all of my heart, but my mind wanders.

I wonder if I will make it out of this house alive.

He's been using me as a stress reliever for six months now and things are getting worse.

I know he loves me, he's just having a rough time right now. If I can just behave myself and control my mouth like he says, then things will get better.

He wasn't always this way.

Justin and I started dating two years ago. He was the nerdy type guy who grew up with both parents in the home. He rarely dated girls because, his parents were so strict on him. They made sure his main focus was on his studies.

Justin went to the best schools. He practically had everything handed to him. He was in the best youth programs, even serving on the Boy' s State Choir at the age of 12.

He never really had to work hard for anything. His parents were there to support him with anything. They loved that he was finically stable.

I, on the other hand, was totally the opposite. My dad died when I was 12, and my mom wasted no time getting another man in the house.

For some reason, a woman sometimes feels somewhat incomplete without a significant other, so they accept any man that comes her way.

This new attraction in my mom' s life is a family "terminator" and I have no idea why she married him. I wonder why she puts up with all the strife he causes her.

You know his type, the type of man who moves into the woman's house and causes havoc within a well-established family.

Maybe he acts the way he does because, he feels like he doesn't fit it since he's not our biological father. I've always told my mom, a good man helps build, not tear down.

Whatever his problems was, he made sure she was always in the middle of them.

He'd complain about us and we'd complain about him. There was always a battle going on in mom's house. My sisters and I had to give up on the old and accept the new household rules.

I was the one who could no longer accept them, so I moved out.

At the age twelve, I decided to move with my paternal

grandmother. She was so sweet and caring. It almost seemed surreal.

She was the biggest church-goer I knew, attending church at least three days a week.

I didn't mind going to church with her. I loved spending time with a "mom" who really cared and wanted me around!

Grandma basically raised me with an iron fist. She made sure I finished high school, she was very proud of me when I walked across the stage to receive my high school diploma.

Grandma was always teaching me about life situations and issues. She would say that age comes with life, but maturity is something that is acquired and wisdom is something that is sought after.

Grandma gave me everything I needed, and some of what I wanted when she had it to give. I was the only grandchild who was close to her, and that gave me the opportunity of having a chance to be there for her as well. We were two peas in a pod. She would take me everywhere she went.

We would even dress alike at the church's annual mother and daughter's tea. I truly loved the way she took me in and taught me what it was like to be a young lady.

Sure I had my teenage issues, but Grandma taught me how to handle and approach them. She never wanted to see me down.

Just a little after my twentieth birthday, grandma passed away. I never got the chance to tell her good-bye. She had kept her illness from me for over three years.

I couldn't understand why she would do such a thing. I couldn't understand why she wouldn't give me the chance to prepare myself for her having to leave me.

Grandma knew how sick she was so, she made sure that when she passed, I would be off to a good start.

She had three insurance policies; one to bury her, one to pay off her house and one just for me.

I was to go to college with some of the money. I just never found it within myself to carry it out. Depression had me down and the grief had set in.

I loved her even more, because in her dying years, she took the time to think of me.

Yet with all the money she left me I still wasn't happy. She was gone and that bothered me.

I felt like my life was over. The pain of losing someone you love so much, was consuming me. I had no one, my biggest supporter and confidant was gone.

I began to turn to other things to take away the pain. I

started smoking marijuana, drinking, and partying. Using anything to numb the heartache and to get me through the day.

I blew through three thousand dollars in one weekend partying and shopping with my friends. I hit rock bottom that weekend. I drank so much.

I passed out in the club and my friend Amber had to rush me to the emergency room.

The doctor said I had drank too much alcohol and suffered from alcohol poisoning. I could have died. After sobering up, I made vow to myself to stop the wild behavior.

Besides, if overdrinking wasn't a wake-up call, I don't know what was.

Still, I could not come to accept the realization I had just lost the only person who really cared about me.

You see, I knew my mother loved me, but caring was totally different.

That's where Justin came in the picture. I met Justin while accompanying Amber to her job's Christmas Party at George E. Waterman Investments Company.

A fairly large investment firm which deals with stocks, bonds and hedge funds among other things.

Justin was a stockbroker who worked at the firm as well. He was the type of person which captured your very soul. He spoke to me and I glanced at him, giving him the look that said, "Get at me".

The next work day, he sent word through Amber he wanted to take me out. I guess my look worked, as if it had ever failed.

We started dating, and soon took things to a whole new level. I must say he was my first real love, He was my first everything.

I had nobody at the time, but Justin was there for me. He brought me anything I needed and then some.

I was twenty-one when we started dating. I never had a real birthday party, so for my twenty-second birthday Justin planned a surprise birthday party for me at the 20/20 Club, Atlanta's hottest and most expensive club.

Justin had plenty of money, his base salary was $90,000 a year plus bonuses which easily pushed him to six figures.

Amber told me Justin had an excellent outcome in trading bringing in well over one hundred twenty-five thousand dollars for the firm. Justin had class, style and charm.

I'd been around his parents three times. He told me his dad was the reason he got into trading.

When we started dating, Justin had just gotten out of a two year relationship. His ex-girlfriend moved to Florida to take care of her ailing mom.

Justin decided to move in with me after his apartment lease was up.

I know that if Grandma were living, she would be against shacking up. I'm sure she would want me to be married first, but Justin said he wanted to take our relationship to the next level. Plus he would be saving two thousand dollars a month in rent.

Justin's best friend, Cain is a real chick magnet. He and Justin met in private school, but Cain was thrown out after his second year due to monetary issues.

Justin's parents helped Cain get back into school by paying Cain's tuition for his entire junior and senior years.

Justin and Cain at times tend to be very heavy with clubbing, leaving Justin to get into trouble with work.

I told him all the time, that clubbing was meant to be on the weekends.

Nonetheless, I was in love with Justin. I was his queen and he was my king.

I felt like I was on top of the world when it came to him. Nothing and no one could separate us.

"Faith, Faith, do you hear me talking to you", Justin questions? "I'm so sorry for everything I've been doing lately, please forgive me".

I look up and Justin's head is in his hands as if he's really sorry this time. I'm holding my head.

I'm holding my head due to the pain, and he's holding his head in disgust, as if he realizes what he's doing is hurting me. He looks at me, sighs and begins explaining.

Justin tells me that things aren't going well with business. With the stock market down, he was forced to liquidate most of his own personal stocks, because of margin calls which he had thousands of dollars in. He also lost over a dozen clients.

He says not to worry. Cain has a special connection who will loan him personal funds, which should help him get back up on his feet.

He tells me it's a waiting game for now and with the new investments the stakes are high and there are still consequences with the stock market.

I think to myself, either way, his personal and business issues doesn't give him the right to take his stress and anger out on me.

Do I forgive him? Of course I do!

I decide to stay. Besides, he's just having problems and no

one should walk away from the person they love because of a problem.

I unpack my bag and go to take a bath. Justin joins me. He touches me, my body, my mind and my soul!

What would I do without him? What would he do without me? I decide to be his everything, besides never leave a man when he's down!

Later that night Justin tells me his dreams of one day marrying me and having a family.

I'm so happy, hopefully, things will turn out fine. I know grandma would have wanted to see me marry and have children. If only she were here, but I know her prayers still live on.

I give Justin a big hug and tell him that everything is going to be okay. Boy, oh boy do I love this man.

2
Waking Up
Breathless

I woke up this morning, feeling like a million bucks. I'm so happy and relieved that Justin was able to discuss with me some of his problems. I always tell him that communication is the key to a successful relationship.

Having that talk was good, because now we can focus on moving forward. Hopefully, we can get our relationship back on track.

Justin's still asleep, so I head into the kitchen to clean up and fix us breakfast.

I wake up Justin with breakfast in bed. He gives me a big hug. Today's going to be a great day, much better than yesterday. I can feel it.

I decide to get out of the house, but where can I go with my face all jacked up? Makeup and sun glasses it is!

I'm all decked out, no worries, especially since Justin and I had a touching night. I think

I'll go to the market to get something good for us to eat for dinner. Maybe steak, shrimp, rice and steamed veggies. I make my market list and head out.

Plus, I think it's only right if I stop at the WestPoint Mall to grab something special from Victoria's "Hush-Hush".

I grab everything I need from the market to make this night special and head to the mall. On my way to the car I saw Darrin.

Darrin was one of my closest friend when I was in high school. I didn't like hanging out with females, because it was way too much drama. So, I hung out with Darrin and his friends most of the time.

Darrin asked me to spend a little time with him to catch up since he hasn't seen me in quite some time. We decided to go grab a bite at the Paper Moon.

Darrin tells me he met a nice woman who's caring, loving and has an outstanding personality. He decided to make their relationship official and marry her.

Well, all his good news, has got me to thinking. I'm thinking; there's no way in the world I tell him what's really going on with me. So, lies, lies, and more lies I decided to tell.

That's when the questions began. The first question he asks is, why did I still have on sunglasses in the mall?

I told him that I was in a bad neighborhood when I was robbed and hit in the face. I go on and on. He just looks in awe, and tells me to make sure I'm careful in certain areas.

We decide to end our lunch date. I need to get home and get things in order for Justin. Me and Darrin arrange a date and time for us to discuss a few business options.

I'm really hoping that this will help me with getting a few of goals started. I have put everything on hold for Justin lately that I forgot to think about myself.

I have to be careful with scheduling my business dates since Justin didn't understand my friendship with Darrin, so he really doesn't want us around each other. I guess he was jealous to some extent.

He thought Darrin was a guy I used to date.

All to make a statement, he stopped me from talking to him. It hurt me, but it was time for me to live my life with Justin, besides, Darrin understood and he still loves me.

I get back in the house and Justin's gone. I'm kind of glad, because I want to get everything together and surprise him. I cook the food and put it in the oven to keep warm.

I call Justin to see what time he will be in the house, so I can be dressed in my "secrets".
There's no answer. This is not like him.

I call again, still no answer. Okay, I've called like ten times in less than five minutes.

I began to panic, what if something bad happened to him? I calm down and began to think positive. Hopefully, he's on his way home and has his music playing too loud in the car and can't hear his phone.

Maybe he left his cell phone in the car and he's standing outside of it or maybe his phone is in vibrate mode and he can't hear it. I wonder where he is.

Twenty minutes goes by, so I call again and still no answer. His phone rings, but goes to the answering machine.

Why isn't he answering? Is he doing this on purpose?

I give up calling for a while. A half hour goes by···this is killing me.

Justin would have returned my calls by now, especially since I've called him so many times.

I decide to call his mom, but, she doesn't answer for me either. I decide to jump in the car and ride pass a few of his friend's houses'.

Before I could put on my jacket, the phone rings it is Justin's mom calling me back.

"Hello Mrs. Romaine, I was just wondering if you saw Justin today", I said before she could even get out her hello.

She did, he was there earlier during the day. She claims to have just gotten off the phone with him about five minutes ago.

"Is he okay", I ask?

"He sounds okay", she said. Oh, maybe that's the reason why he didn't answer my calls. I thought I would give you a call since it's not like Justin not to answer his phone for me.

"Good bye Faith", his mom said abruptly.

"Good bye ma' am".

I hang up the phone and called Justin again. Still no answer.

I began to wonder what his problem may be, what's making him not want to talk to me.

I'll just wait. Maybe he's busy. As long as I know he's okay, I'm fine.

I head off to the kitchen, looking my best. I sit down to relax myself and get me a drink of my favorite, Moscoto Peach. Not too much, but just enough to get a buzz.

I began to think of what I'm going to do for Justin's 29th birthday next month.

Six o' clock rolls around, eight 0' clock, then ten 0' clock, still no Justin. I fall asleep, well, I cry myself to sleep. All this I went through to make this night special and he's not here. He better have a good excuse.

5AM a rolls around, I'm awaken up from my sleep after hearing the door slam.

Justin comes in the room, takes off his clothes.

I look at him as if to say, where's my explanation?

Better yet, where's the respect coming in the house five o' clock in the morning?

He says nothing. This isn't like him.

I don't say anything to him. I just look in disgust. I turn over and just stare into space.

"I'm sorry for getting in so late", he finally says. I was taking care of business.

Business, I think to myself? Business has never had me worry about him all night. I'm starting to see the big picture here.

The only things that have a man out all night and not answering his phone are bars and opened legs and he sure doesn't smell like alcohol!

I still try to continue to trust him.

I say nothing, I'm thinking about what happens if I do; like the slap I'll get if open my mouth.

I just want a peace of mind. I need a piece of faith. There has to be something that will get us through this trial. I know that once we get through this, it will make us stronger.

I fall asleep in his arms.

I'm abruptly woken by a phone call. It's my mom, she tells me my youngest sister, Lisa has been hit by a car and they are on their way to the hospital.

She tells me to come to the hospital for a family meeting. A family meeting; this doesn't sound good to me?

The last time I went to a family meeting, it was to inform us my grandma wouldn't pull through her illness.

I get dressed and head to the hospital. Justin decides to stay home to get rest since he's been out all night. He tells me to call him if I need him.

At the hospital, the doctor tells us Lisa is in bad shape. They put her in a medically induced coma and she's in critical condition. Lisa has massive brain trauma and the next twenty-four to forty-eight hours could be very crucial.

The doctor starts Lisa's treatment and hope she will respond, but even if she does, they are not certain of her outcome.

Mom is beside herself. I sit unresponsive; numb at the pain of hearing and witnessing this whole ordeal and hurt that my sister is suffering. Not to mention her uncertain future. She doesn't deserve this, but who does?

We have been through so much in our childhood and now this.

I called Justin as he insisted, but he doesn't answer the phone. "Thanks for being here for me and my family. You think you're going through something, try walking in my shoes", I yelled sarcastically in the phone!

At this moment I've had enough.

I reflect on what grandma told me. You're a strong person; you can conquer anything.

"Grandma, if only I had you here with me", I whisper.

There was a time when everything in my life was coming together. Now it seems like it's falling apart.

Visiting hours are coming to an end, so I decided to say my good nights to Lisa.

Afterwards, I head out into the hallway. I give Michele, my next youngest sister a hug.

My mom approaches us and gives us malevolent stare. Here it comes, I thought to myself.

Mom had the nerve to lash out and tell us we are to blame for Lisa's behavior.

"Lisa was trying to run away, and your stepdad was trying to stop her", she says.

I say nothing, but Michele isn't all that lenient on mom.

Michele speaks up, "Don't blame us for anything, you

should, however blame our problems, on your husband" !

What and/or who made Lisa run away? I thought. What happened at home to make her want to run away that badly? Better yet, was someone chasing her?

I needed to get to the bottom of things. When Lisa makes it through, she won't be going back there.

I pull Michele away from mom with that look mom had on her face, Michele was about to get it. I tell her this is neither the time nor the place.

I left the hospital well after visiting hours. Lisa was still hanging in there. I'm thankful for that.

I wasn't able to sit in the room too long with her because only two visitors were allowed at a time, so we took turns. She's a tough cookie and I believe she will pull through.

I arrived home only to find Justin's not there. I head up stairs to get myself ready for bed. I'm so tired and that's all I want to do right now, since I have a mental overload.

I think I may have an ulcer due to stressing. My stomach has been hurting me for the past two weeks. I'll have to make sure I call my doctor tomorrow and make an appointment.

I get out the shower, and Justin's standing in the bathroom waiting. "What's your problem Faith", he says. I totally ignore him; rolling my eyes. He knows what my problem is. He should have been there for me.

He looks at me, turns around and punches me in the chest. I fly back into the wall. He hits me so hard, I can hardly breathe. He comes over to me and slaps me in the face, yelling about how he's tired of my nagging.

I gather my breath and pick myself up off the floor. Justin's standing in front of me. I look at him tell him what a cheap blow that was and if he's tired, then he should leave.

For the first time in six months I felt like I stood up for myself.

Justin looks at me, takes his hands, puts them around my neck and tells me he will never leave me, but I can leave him, in a body bag.

I wake up the next morning still in shock from the critical news and blows I received yesterday.

My main focus today is my sister, she comes first. As soon as visiting hours begin, I plan to be there.

However, I'm not feeling well right now. I feel really faint and my chest is hurting from the blow last night. I ran to the bathroom to vomit. When I came out I realize Justin's not here, he must have left out early.

I put my clothes on and head out the door. On my way out I see Justin. He's standing down the street with Taylor. Taylor is a neighbor, one of which I don't associate with. I don't know this girl, she just moved into the area about six months ago.

Justin sees me, but acts as if he's really into the

conversation, perhaps he is. I walk over to the both of them and stand in the middle. Taylor is surprised by my actions, but Justin seems to be unmoved.

"Hey, what's going on", I ask.

"Not much", says Justin.

He tells Taylor he will talk to her later. She just nods and turns, eyeing me at the same time. I give her the look that says, "Try me".

"What was that about", I ask Justin?

He claims it's nothing. She was just asking him about the area and who's who. I look at him and ask him if he was the neighborhood "Information person" now? He doesn't answer me, he stands there looking stupid.

I tell him I'm on my way out and I would see him later. "How long are you going to be", he asks? Not too long I tell him.

After witnessing the interaction between Justin and Taylor, I will definitely be on guard.

3
Wake Up Call

I decide to give Darrin a call today. I really need someone to talk to. Darrin's out and about. I ask him if he's busy. Never too busy for you he tells me. He said he was happy that I called him.

Darrin, informs me he has to meet with his cousin, Kevin later. I know Kevin "very well", he and I went to the prom together. Darrin asks me to meet him at Kevin's house. We can talk there.

I head to the hospital to check on Lisa. Even though my mom made me out to be the bad guy for not liking her significant other, I decide to support my family regardless.

I arrive at the hospital. The doctor informs us Lisa is taking the treatment well, but is still in critical condition, but so far so good.

I sit with my mom and sister for a while in the waiting room. I pull out my book and began to read a little. My mom comes over to me and tells me her attitude towards me is my fault, because I refuse to give my stepdad a chance.

She even had the audacity to say I put wedge between our relationships. The nerve!

I inform her, very nicely, that her choice of marrying a man who causes strife with her children is the "wedge" she sees, not me. I get up and walk away. At this point the only interaction I want to have with my mom is slim to none.

I go to check on Lisa one last time before I leave to meet Darrin. As I look at my sister and the tears starts to flow down my face. My heart aches heavily watching my little sister lie there helplessly.

I give Lisa a kiss on her hand and head out.

I arrive at Kevin's house to meet Darrin. This is risky, if Justin finds out, it could mean big trouble. However, I don't care; I needed someone I can trust.

Kevin answers the door. He pulls me in the house and hugs me tight. I feel comforted, because I know I'm amongst good caring friends.

Darrin comes to the door grabs me and gives me an even bigger hug.

"Can I get you anything to drink Faith", Kevin asks?

"I am a little thirsty, do you have any iced tea", I respond?

"Anything for you missy", he adds.

I breathe a sigh of relief and smile.

Kevin takes me on a tour of his new house.

"Wow, Kevin, I love how you decorated the place", I say as he hands me my tea.

He thanks me and looks at me with a very soft sincere smile. Then he heads out the door, giving me and

Darrin time to talk. He says he will be back.

My phone rings, it's Justin, but I don't answer. I send him straight to voicemail.

Darrin asks how have things been since we last spoke. Before I could answer him, I broke down and cried.

I could no longer hold in all the frustration, hurt and pain.

"Faith, tell me what's wrong, I'm here for you, honey".

I began to tell Darrin all the problems I've been having. I tell him everything, but I didn't tell him about Justin's hand problem. That was just too embarrassing and I knew Darrin wouldn't take it lightly.

In order to keep the peace between everyone, I held back that one piece of information.

Darrin gives me some pretty good advice. He tells me about his business deal with his electronics store expansion and tells me he needed a good employee to run the service department. He asked me if I would like to work for him.

Now in no way shape or form did I think I would be qualified to run his service department. I shared this information with him.

However, he said he would send me to school to get me certified and prepared. I tell him I would think about it and give him a call within a week.

Before we left, Darrin tells me about his issues he's having with his fiancée', Jennifer, regarding setting a wedding date.

"You have to meet her", Darrin said. "You'll love her", she's smart, funny, and straightforward", he adds.

I tell him maybe the next time we meet, he can bring her so we can become acquainted. At this stage in my life I need a positive person to lean on.

I get up to leave and Darrin looks at me again and asks, "Are you okay"?

"Yes, I'm fine", I answered.

"Anything in life that has worth isn't easy to get. You must move forward to attain it", said Darrin.

I just smiled.

I head home, this time Justin's in the house. "Where have you been"? I called your phone several times and no answer.

"Well, I guess you know how it feels when someone you're trying to get a hold of doesn't answer the phone on purpose", I said very nicely.

I'm waiting for his rage, but this time it doesn't come. Instead, Justin asks me to borrow some of the money grandma left me

from the insurance policy. He says
he needs the money for the deal with
Cain.

> I tell him I don't work, so
> if I give him the money and
> it's a bust I'm in big
> trouble. Besides I've
> learned my lesson with
> excessive spending.

Justin begins acting irrational.
He begins telling me he's done
anything and everything for me, so
why can't I give back to him?

> "Why can't you ask your
> parents for the money? They
> have more money than me and
> they are a very good support
> system for you", I tell him.

He tells me his mom refuses to
help him in anyway, because he
chooses to be with me a little low-
life female who wants nothing out
of life.

> I'm crushed. I never thought
> in a million years that his mom felt
> that way. I never would have thought

she would make such a preference in who Justin dates.

   We've been together for three years and she has never said anything to me.

   "Why am I just hearing about this", I ask him?

Justin looks stupid because, he let the cat out of the bag.

   "You didn't mean for me to find out that your mom doesn't care for me, because she thinks I'm worthless", I question?

Justin tries to explain to me that his parents only want the best for him.

   I tell Justin that he couldn't possibly have told his parents anything about me as a person, because I have only wanted the best for him.

   "Are you going to give me the money? I don't want to talk about it. I just need to know if you're going to give me the money", he screams?

"How much money do you need", I ask?

"Ten thousand", he responds.

I say nothing for a moment.

"I need time to think about this", I say.

"Think, think about what", Justin shouts!

"I need to know if we're going to be okay. What if things don't pull through", I ask?

"What, you don't trust me? Besides what about everything I've done for you, and for us", Justin says?

I can see the anger in his eyes.

"I will check my bank account tomorrow to see how much money I can give you", I said all to avoid another beating.

Even still, after hearing this Justin grabs me by my neck and balls up his fist, but I'm not afraid this time.

"Do it, do it", I yell!

He lets me go and tells me I'd better get the money, especially after all he's has given me.

I head into the bathroom, frustrated by all the problems and issues going on in my life right now. Half of what I've been through would not be, if only she had been here with me.

If only God didn't take her from me. Couldn't He just give me a few more years with my grandmother?

Doesn't he care enough to see what I've been through and cut me some slack?

I open the medicine cabinet, take out the pain pills, pour a bunch in my hand, and look at myself in the mirror.

I've had enough. I've had enough with the crying and the feelings of betrayal, disrespect, and animosity. I can't take this any longer.

Everything is falling apart; I'm falling apart. I put the pills in my mouth and turn on the faucet.

I can't do it, I can't follow through. I began to think logically and I hear grandma's voice within, "What are you doing Faith"? "These things you're going through are not to hurt you, but to help you".

I spit the pills out and push myself against the wall; I slide down to the floor. "Is this what it feels like when your back is up against the wall", I ask myself? Besides, what type of help does a person get from pain and suffering?

I wake up this morning, my stomach is aching and I need to vomit. I ran to the bath room with my head in the toilet and then I remember.

With all the drama going on I didn't even noticed a missed period. I call my doctor to make an appointment. I will grab a pregnancy test from the store.

This may be my reason for the nausea.

I get myself ready to leave, Justin's still in the bed. He asks me to join him back in bed. "I'm sorry for everything and I can't be sorry enough", Justin adds.

We have a touching moment. He tells me how he wants everything to be okay with us. How it used to be when we first dated. He said how he was sorry for his parent's behavior towards me and explained why he never told me how his mom really felt.

As I sat listening to Justin, I realize just how much our relationship means to me. However, I just couldn't understand why he's treating me so bad.

I couldn't understand how he didn't see that I'm here to support him and not make things worse. Normally, we're able to talk about anything. However now days, it's like we're so far apart.

While I have Justin's attention, I decide to tell him I haven't had a period in a month and a half.

"So you might be pregnant", Justin asks?

"Yes", I respond.

I explain to him I have been feeling sick lately and this may be the reason why.

Justin takes my hand and places it on his chest. "This changes everything", he whispers to himself.

I say nothing, thinking the change he means is the change in his behavior.

"Are you excited", I ask?

"Well, first we'll have to see if you are or aren't", he says.

"I'll grab a pregnancy test from the pharmacy store when I come from seeing Lisa.

"You are going to go to the bank today, right", Justin asks.

"Sure", I answer him.

"Good girl", says Justin.

4
Waking Up Little
By Little

I decide to take Darrin up on his offer and run the service department at his Electronics Store. I remember him saying his vision for his store was to one day is to be as big as Best Buy and Radio Shack.

I would like to be a part of his dream. Not to mention, it gives me good reason to go to college and get on the right track. I'm hoping Justin's parents will be satisfied with me going to college.

First things first, this morning, checking in on my baby sister. We still haven't found out why Lisa was trying to run away from home.

I decide to talk to my stepdad. He's been at the hospital every day since Lisa has been in there. We may not like each other, but hopefully he'll give more information than my mom.

I walk into the hospital's waiting room, Michele's already there. She tells me Lisa moved her hand for the first time today after the accident. "That's great, this means she's responding", I asked?

Michele tells me no, not really, it could be a response like a nerve tremor. Just as I'm heading into Lisa's room, I find they have asked her family to exit her room. I began to panic.

"What's wrong, my mom asks?

The doctor tells us, they have started to withdraw Lisa from the medically induced coma. The next step is to see how she handles it.

I don't know what to do and I don't know what's going on. We think the worse.

I can't breathe I'm having an anxiety attack and I'm feeling nauseous. I head to the bathroom. I go into the stall and for the first time in three years, I start to pray.

I haven't talked to God in three years, because I didn't understand why he would take my grandmother away from me. He knew she was the only person who really loved me.

I prayed for Lisa, my family issues and I prayed for myself. Grandma always said to contend for the faith. She said with faith, all things are possible.

Michele comes in the bathroom to get me.

"Faith, come hurry up, she yelled, it's Lisa" !

I rush out of the bathroom and into Lisa's room. Lisa's gagging for air as if she's trying to breath. I look at her, she's disorientated, but that's okay, she's breathing on her own!

The doctors inform us Lisa still needs much rest and treatment. She has a long road of recovery ahead of her; full with rehabilitation. They ask if we would only stay a couple of minutes.

We all head back to the waiting room. We're all so excited. I decide not to ask my stepdad what happened the night Lisa was hit by the car. This was not the time.

Anyway, if Lisa remembers, she can tell me herself. She's awake now and I feel at peace with knowing that!

I have so much other things to do today like stop by the pharmacy store and bank.

On my way home from the hospital I receive a call from Darrin. He asks me how Lisa's coming along. I couldn't wait to tell him the good news.

I inform him I would love to take him up on his job offer.

He's excited and relieved I'll be taking the job. Plus, I will be helping him achieve his dreams; all awhile I'm helping myself with mine.

We decide to meet up at Kevin's house later tonight to discuss the job further.

I know today will be a good day!

My thoughts go back to being pregnant. I can't accept having a baby right now. Our relationship is way too perplexed already. I couldn't imagine bringing such a precious gift into this world given our circumstances.

After my errands, I'll go visit Amber. She is my closet friend and we share everything with each other.

I haven't been around Amber much in the past six months, because I didn't want her to suspect or know about my problems with Justin.

Before I visit her, I decide to go home to take the pregnancy test. I stop past the bank and get a cashier's check made out for Justin.

Things will be pretty tight now, until he gets on his feet. I'm glad I decided to take the job with Darrin.

I get home, and again Justin's not here. I pay it no mind that he's not home. Actually, I'm quite glad, because it gives me a peace of mind.

It's hard dealing with someone who's not happy with themselves. They become miserable and want everyone around them miserable.

I head to the bathroom to take the test. I'm worried about what this will mean if the test is positive. One minute goes by and it seems like one year, another minute and another year. Plus sign!

I drop my head and began to cry. I'm 23 years old, no degree, no job and no goals. I can just imagine what grandma would be saying right now. Well, I don't even want to imagine the things she'd be saying.

I'm at a standstill and I need to get out of the house. I decide to walk the eight blocks to Amber's house to get some fresh air. Besides, I haven't been outside in a minute, with all the hiding I do. I don't want anyone to see my scars or marks. I refresh my make-up and head to Amber's house.

I get to the corner and notice Justin's car parked between the alley and the side of Taylor's house. Now I know Justin's not home, so why would his car be parked here?

I call his phone, but no answer. I call three more times, still no answer. I text him and tell him I'm at the bank and need to ask him a quick question about the money. He texts me back and ask me to give him 5 minutes.

I cross the street and stand on the other corner, so he would not see me when he walked to his car.

My heart is pounding and I feel faint right now. What am I going to do if this man steps out of this woman's house? First and foremost, I don't fight over any man. Whatever problem I have with a man is with the man.

I always say, if you're in a relationship, that relationship should be identified as to what type of relationship each participant wants. As far as I know, our relationship does not include extras.

This should exclude cheating, if it's a relationship that has been identified as a monogamist one. This is the decision we made with our relationship and now he's broken our agreement.

Whatever I face at this moment, I decided to be like Mary J. Blige and show Justin that I'm not going to cry. I've learned by now he likes getting me in a position where I feel helpless.

I text Justin back again, hoping to hurry him. I'm anxious to know if Taylor is the reason for Justin's short temperament with me.

Wow! Justin steps on the porch with Taylor behind him. I began to walk up to the porch. Justin's back is turned as he gives Taylor a good-bye hug.

As I approach, Taylor sees me coming. She lets Justin go and Justin turns around to see me standing there.

It takes everything in me to hold back from acting like a fool. Nonetheless, I stand my ground and I'm not going to lower my standards. I'm going to hit him where it hurts.

"So this affair is the reason for your perfidious behavior", I ask?

He stands there looking in silence.

Taylor starts talking, "I'm not sorry for the things happening between me and Justin, I'm just sorry you found out about us this way. I asked Justin to tell you the truth a long time ago".

"Is that right", I ask?

Taylor looks at me dumb founded by my response. I guess she's looking for some type of wild and unseemly behavior from me, but that's not happening.

Never let them see you sweat!

Justin turns around and tells her to go in the house. Before she closes the door I tell her that she's crazy if she thinks his going to have a relationship with him.

He doesn't know the meaning of commitment.

"Whatever little girl", Taylor yells!

"As a matter of fact, if I wasn't pregnant I would drag you up and down this street", I respond.

I could feel my temper rising. Plus I just had to let her know we're having a baby.

"Oh and by the way Justin, you're not getting a dime from me, get it from her", I shouted!

Justin looked at me as if he could kill me. I just turned and walked away.

Now, there's no way in the world I was going to head home. I knew if he ever got me alone, he would just beat on me.

I continue to head to Amber's house as fast as I could. Justin runs and grabs me.

"Taylor is nobody, she means nothing to me", he shouts!

Taylor, who's looking out the side window of her house, overhears Justin. She opens her window.

"Justin, you didn't say that 10 minutes ago when you were in my bed", she shouts!

I stop walking and look at Justin as if nobody and nothing else matters at the moment.

"You've hurt me for the last time", I tell him.

Justin stood there frozen and looking dumb founded.

"Faith, you've got to believe me", she's nothing to me and I'm sorry".

Taylor stood there looking stupid not saying a word after Justin repeated himself. On that note, I looked up at her and gave her a smirk look. What a silly chick I thought.

It's always these desperate women out here letting any and every man lay-up with them. Don't they know desperation leads to error?

On that note, I turn and walk away from Justin.

As I walk away I decide to go home. I didn' t want Amber to know just how much pain I was in. Besides, I' ve kept everything from her this far. I didn' t want her judging me anyway.

I couldn' t believe this. All types of things are running through my head right now. I turned the corner to go the opposite direction and heard the screeching tires from Justin' s car.

Get in the car Faith he begins to yell out the window like a crazy person.

I ignore him.

"Get in the car Faith" ,

Justin yelled louder.

Still, I ignore him as if he wasn' t talking to me.

Ignoring people was one of my mastered skills. I learned to do it when I was living with my mom and stepdad.

The more Justin yelled, the more I look forward. I'm sure this confuses him. He's unsure of what I would do right now.

My heart is telling me that all people make mistakes and my mind is telling me to throw his clothes and belongings out the door when I get home.

Maybe I should go into a "Waiting to Exhale" mode and burn his nice "top of the line" suits. That thought brought a smile to my face, but I don't like handcuffs. I won't be going to jail for destruction of property.

I arrive home and stood at the bottom of the steps and look at the door. Then I look at Justin as he's parking his car. I could see the evil in his eyes and the fake tears flowing from his face, while still calling my name.

I turn again and look at the door again. My life flashes before

my eyes. If I enter into this place,
I might not make it out alive.

I made a quick dash to my car.
I jumped in and sped off. As I look
in the mirror, I could see Justin
running after me. Then he stops as
I reach the end of the block.

5
Waking Up from a
Nightmare

My phone rings, it's Justin. I don't answer it. He calls again and again, but I let the phone go to voicemail.

I listen to one of the messages. He's saying he's sorry and he messed up. He wants to be with me and the baby.

I pull over, should I go back and let him explain? Maybe he's learned his lesson. Many thoughts race through my mind.

I call Darrin, but he doesn't answer. So I head over to Kevin's house to see if I can track him down.

I get to Kevin's house, but Darrin's car is not there. Kevin answers the door from my frantic knock. He looks at me and pulls me in the house.

"What's the matter Faith?
"What's wrong", he says as he holds me?

All my fears, frustration and resentment seem to have departed. I tell Kevin I don't want to talk about it, but he insists and I resist. I tell him I just need time to get away to think.

"I'm just having man troubles", I tell him.

He looks at me and says,

"I've always known you to be a strong woman, you're beautiful and your personality is to die for. You don't get this with all women.

I try to take the attention off of me for a moment.

"Can I get something to drink", I ask?

"Anything for you Faith", he says.

"I hope I'm not interrupting any of your plans, I was looking for Darrin".

"Darrin went to a business workshop in New York for the weekend". "He might not be available by phone right now, but you have me", he adds.

I just smile.

However, my mind takes me back to Justin along with the many phone calls which keep coming in from him. I turn off my phone.

"So are you going to tell me the truth about what's bothering you and why you ran over to my house looking for Darrin", Kevin asks?

"Like I said, I'm having man problems", I answer with a fake grin.

Kevin looks at me with suspicion.

"So why don't you have a girlfriend", I asked Kevin trying to avoid any questions from him?

"I've dated a few, but they always turned up either interested in money and/or material things. None of

which were sincere about
real love".

He looks in my eyes and says
real love doesn't come as
straightforward as he hoped.
Therefore, he tends to wait.

The doorbell rings. "I'm
not expecting anyone", Kevin
says.

He goes to the door. I can
hear a man's voice. It sounds
like Justin. I walk to the
vestibule and my heart drops,
it's Justin.

He's furious and I'm frantic.
"You followed me here", I
asked?

"Do you want to do this
here Faith? Here in front of
your little boyfriend? Is
the baby even mine", Justin
begins to go off?

"What are you talking
about, don't put this on
me, you're the one
cheating", I shouted!

Kevin interrupts and asks Justin to leave his property right now or suffer the consequences.

Justin tells me either I leave with him now, or else.

Kevin tells him that I don't have to go anywhere if I don't want to. They come eye to eye with each other.

I didn't think Justin would back down from Kevin given his need to always hit on me. Nonetheless, he did.

I stand between them and tell Kevin I apologize for bringing this commotion to his house and more over involving him in this chaos.

Justin grabs me by the arm and slightly pushes me out the door. As Kevin watches us as we leave. I see Kevin grab his keys and coat.

I decide to go home with Justin. We really needed to talk things out.

As soon as we get in the house Justin slaps me. The next time I call you and you don't come, it's more where that came from", he says forcefully. He slaps me again.

"The next time I call your phone and you don't answer, I will hunt you down and kill you", he adds.

He grabs me by my neck and the thoughts of dying run through my mind.

Then he says to me softly kissing my lips with his right hand around my throat, "I was trying to make things right".

He kisses me again.

"So tell me, who's this guy you ran to", he asked?

"Why Taylor, I asked?

"Taylor is a low life female who holds a high regard for money. She means absolutely nothing to me. She would never be a girl of mine. I was feeling very low and in despair over work issues so, I ventured out. I never meant to hurt you. She means nothing and that's that", he said.

"Kevin is Michele's friend, I was looking for Michele", I start explain.

"Why are you lying to me Faith", he asks?

"What are you talking about, please believe me Justin, I'm telling you the truth. I would never cheat on you", I said.

"Kevin is Darrin's friend, the one you went to the prom with. Your first, oh what you forgot you told me about him. I can see the passion you still have for him in your eyes." Justin screams?

"I would never cheat on you, Justin, I love you so much", I start crying.

"You've been sneaking over to Kevin's house for over the past few weeks. I put a GPS on your car and his place seems to keep being your choice of destination. You've been seeing him", said Justin?

"I have not, I only went to meet Darrin, he wanted to discuss business, it's nothing more", I tell Justin.

"Is this why you don't want to give me the money, because you're going into business with Darrin", he questions?

"No, it was because of Taylor, it's because of you", I shouted!

Before I could say another word out of my mouth Justin jumps up and punches me right in the stomach. I'm bent over in severe pain. Then he takes me by my hair and yells,

"You're not going to give me the money"?

I start yelling and screaming, because something inside of me knew I was in trouble. I tried to fight back. It took all of my might to release my hair from his hands, but still no luck.

I reach up and scratch him in the face trying my best to take out an eye. He's fed up; and uses all of his might to throw me across the room.

Then walks over to me and kicks me in the face. Just then, the front door is kicked in.

It's Kevin! Kevin punches Justin. Justin falls on top of the coffee table, breaking it. Kevin gets on top of Justin to try to finish him off.

Justin kicks Kevin off of him. I'm able to finally get up and stand. I try to run to the front door to get help, but Justin sees me.

He somehow gets away from Kevin. He grabs me by my collar and tosses me down the stairs. I hit my head on the hard concrete steps.

Blood runs everywhere, I'm out cold.

6
Waking up to Realization

I see a light shining from the sky as I lay on the front steps of my house. I can't move. Then walking towards me was a shadowy figure. I can't make out who it is due to the bright light.

Finally, as the figure hoovers over me, I see it is grandma.

She bends towards me and once again asks, "What are you doing Faith".

It seems as though these particular words are all I have been imagining grandma saying to me.

"Faith, what are you doing", the figure asks me again?

"I'm not doing anything grandma, I answer. I can't move.

"Exactly, says the figure of grandma. You're living your life bound and it's not the fact of you not being able to move, it's because you won't move. "Get up Faith and move", said the shadowy figure.

"I – I can' t", I began to cry.

"Why"?

"I don' t know", I said softly.

"Because you haven' t let go", said grandma.

"Let go of what", I ask.

"Let go and let God", said grandma

"I don' t understand", I questioned.

"You have not used anything I have taught or demonstrated to you. This is why you' re stuck. All of life' s lessons are teaching tools. You don' t need me to continue to teach you when you have already been taught", says grandma.

"Get up Faith and gather yourself", added grandma.

"I can't! You're all I have. I have no one else. I'd rather just be dead if I'm not already", I mumbled.

Then grey clouds began to form, a bright light began to come down from the sky, and a face started coming through the clouds.

Grandma began to say, "No, she's not ready, no, please she's not ready!

Grandma fades, the clouds formed back and I woke up hearing the sound of people…

"Yes, we have a pulse", I heard someone say!

I black out again. No dream this time, just total darkness.

I woke up hearing someone calling my name.

> "Faith, Faith, you just gotta have a little Faith", it's mom's voice.

I open my eyes, but I could hardly see out of my right eye. Justin had kicked me so hard, my eye was swollen shut. I could see my mom sitting on the edge of my bed, holding my hand.

> "Faith can you hear me squeeze my hand", she asks?

I faintly try to squeeze her hand. I want her to know I could hear and respond to her.

> She begins to cry, "How could I have two daughters sitting in the same hospital at the same time"?

She leans over me and tells me to hang in there.

> I can see Michele. She's just staring at me, with a look of puzzlement. I can't hardly say a

word, my mouth is hurting and I'm in so much pain.

The doctors come in and ask everyone to leave and let me rest. As everyone kisses me and leave the room, I see the police standing outside my door.

I try to remember what happened, but I can't put together all the details.

The police come in the room and ask me if I remember what happened to me tonight. I just turn my head with a no.

Today, I feel a little better, probably because they pumped me full of pain killers. My nurse comes in to check on me. I try to speak. My mouth doesn't hurt as much.

I ask her what happened to me, she says me the ambulance brought me in three days ago suffering from a concussion from a fall. She leaves and I still can see the police sitting outside of my door. "Am I under arrest", I think to myself?

Just then Kevin comes in the room and kisses me on the forehead. I finally can remember some details after seeing his face. I began to cry.

I remember the fight Justin and I had. I remember falling down the stairs and Kevin and Justin fighting, but if Kevin is standing here, then what happened to Justin?

The police detectives come back in to question me.

"Faith", they call out to me. "Yes", I answer.

"This is Detective Malloy and "I'm Lieutenant Randall. We would like to talk to you about the night you had that terrible fall down the stairs", Lieutenant Randall continued?

"Yes sir", I answer as I look at Kevin in the corner of the room.

I didn't want to give any information until after I remember what happened. Besides, only the three people who were there knew what happened. Not now anyway, not until I can remember everything", I answer them.

After the detectives leave Kevin comes over to the bed asking.

"Why didn't you tell them the whole story"?

"I don't know the whole story, I say. Besides if I did would I want to tell"?

"Sure you can, nothing happened after your fall. After you fell down the stairs, I ran after you to help you. Once Justin saw you had been knocked out by the fall, he ran down the stairs and out the house", Kevin said.

"He probably ran to his parent's house", I add.

"I called the ambulance and your mom to meet us at the hospital". Once we got here,

I told her what happened to you and she had the police come. Oh by the way, she gave them the go ahead to press charges on Justin".

"Why would she do that", I interrupt Kevin?

"Why? He could have nearly beaten you to death, if I hadn't come to check on you", Kevin said furiously shaking his head at me.

"No, I'm not saying it as if he doesn't deserve to pay for what he did to me.

I'm glad my mom decided to step up and be supportive of me. I really need her right now.

My mom came in the room. Kevin gave her a hug then left the room giving us time to talk.

Mom looks at me with tears in her eyes. I ask her if she's okay. She assures me, all will be well.

She tells me Lisa is doing great and has been upgraded from critical condition to stable condition. I feel so much better hearing the good news.

The doctor comes in and informs us my CAT scan came back and I should be able to go home in a few days.

He tells me I was lucky I didn't crack my skull or have any severe brain trauma. I have a small fracture in my cervical vertebra and a broken leg. He leaves the bad news for last, I lost my baby.

I should be relieved right now, but I'm not, and I miss Justin. If only I can talk to him. I'm sure we can clear this up. It was all a big misunderstanding.

My mom insists I stay with her until I'm able to get around on my own and Justin is caught. I don't want him caught, I just want to talk to him.

"Faith", my mom says?

"Can we talk, mother to daughter", she adds?

"Sure", I answer her, hoping we don't get into an argument.

She tells me what happened to Lisa, the night she was hit by the car.

She tells me why my stepdad hasn't been around since Lisa woke up. A pparently, Lisa told mom that the night she was hit by the car she and my stepdad were home alone when he came into the bathroom. Lisa says was taking a bath.

She began to yell "get out of here" at him, when he grabbed her by the arm and told her she's going to do what her mother won't do.

Lisa pulled her arm back, grabbed the towel and ran out the bathroom and into her bedroom.

He then tried to get in the room to talk to her, after seeing she would not give in to his affections.

Lisa got dressed and tried to head out of the door. My stepdad then pushed her up against the wall and told her she'd better not tell my mom or else.

Lisa, scared, ran out of the house as fast as she could and right into the path of an oncoming car. At the hospital, my stepdad told my mom that Lisa was trying to run away after an argument they had over Lisa not cleaning her room.

I couldn't believe my ears. The tears were streaming down my face and hers. Mom grabs my hand and asks me to forgive her for allowing someone like him into our home and in her heart.

She admits her wrongs and faults. Then she apologizes for blaming me and Michele.

"Faith, he can't hurt us anymore, Justin won't be able hurt you anymore".

"My soon to be ex-husband has been arrested and charged with assault, child endangerment and child molestation", Mom said with a sigh of relief.

I can tell she's hurting. She really loves him.

I finally came clean and told my mom I had been allowing Justin to physically abuse me over the past six months.

"If we stand by what we believe, no one can ever get away with hurting us again", mom assures me.

"Faith, I want you to tell the police what happened to you and how long it has been going on, please don't continue to allow someone to abuse you. You are precious in every way and can do much better.

I agreed that it was time to take a stand. I allowed the police to take my statement and they issue a warrant for Justin's arrest.

I've been in the hospital for two weeks now and it's time to go. No more police standing outside my door, no more eating this hospital food! I'm ecstatic!

Darrin and his fiancée' arrives.

"I'm glad to finally meet you Jennifer", I said.

"I'm sorry, we had to meet on these terms.

Jennifer gave me a big hug and tells me she's glad to finally meet you. I've heard so much about you. Darrin talks about you all the time.

Kevin and mom finally arrive to pick me up.

"The gangs is all here", mom said.

"Yes, we're all accounted for, but you guys didn't have to go through this much trouble over me. I don't think Justin will try to come and hurt me", I tell them.

"Anything is possible, Faith, said Darrin.

"Right, you never know nowadays. Nobody wants to go to jail and if they are desperate enough they will and can eliminate the one person who can put them there, so it's best to be safe than sorry", Jennifer said.

I guess they're right from a certain standpoint, but I know Justin loves me. Besides, he still thinks I'm carrying his baby. Doesn't that stand for something?

I make my way downstairs. Mom will ride with Kevin, and I will ride with Darrin and Jennifer. We stop by to say hi to Lisa and tell her the good news of her going to rehabilitation soon. She gave me the biggest hug today. I felt one hundred percent better from that hug.

Before we get to mom's house we stop by my house to grab some extra clothes and make sure everything's in order.

I see Justin's handbag and luggage is gone. I guess this means he's gone as well.

Kevin gives me the new key and tells me he had the locks changed. Justin must have gotten his clothes before then. He must be scared right now.

I wonder what he's thinking, but what should I care, and why I'm I still worrying about this man? I have to get him out of my head right now, but I can't.

I check my phone messages, still no Justin. He must be laying low. I'm sure he'll call me.

Jennifer comes up stairs to help me pack.

"How's everything coming along", she asks.

"It's coming, but, can I be honest with you", I ask her?

"Sure, if we're going to be sisters, I want you to feel comfortable talking to me about anything", says Jennifer.

"I'm not taking this all too well. I'm thinking about Justin all the time. I really need to talk to him, so we can get a better understanding of what's going on.

I do realize what he did was wrong, but he's going through so much right now", I said.

"You're not going to be totally freed from Justin at this point, it will take some time and healing. It's not easy, but one day, you will look back at this moment and realize just how strong you're being Faith", she says.

She wipes the tears from my eyes and smiles at me. You'll be just fine and in time will find the right person for you and he just might be right under your nose.

I share with her the dream I had when I blacked out after the fall.

"Faith, I believe your grandmother was trying to send you a message telling you it's time for you to think about everything you're doing with your life".

"I agree, grandma was communicating with me to get me to realize the need to come out of the situations I was allowing to happen in my life. I really need to get myself together. I'm twenty-three years old and have nothing going on for myself", I said.

"Maybe you should attend a support group for women who's battling or suffering from domestic violence. My church has a domestic violence group, put together by an awesome group of women focused on helping those who have been abused. I'll even pick you up and take you since you're unable to drive", Jennifer said.

"Honey, I'm a hot mess, with this neck brace and a cast on my leg", I said.

"I assure you, you'll be just fine", she said, as we both laughed.

It was nice having Jennifer around to talk to. I can see why Darrin loves her so much.

I'm glad he found his soul mate. I'm very happy for the both of them.

I decide at that moment to make a change in my life. If it took going to a church support group to help me get through this it's okay.

I've got to do what, I've got to do and even church can help lead you. There's no harm in that.

I'm sure grandma is smiling down on me at this moment.

I can hear her saying, as she always did, "Getting in trouble is easy, but getting out of trouble is tough.

Grandma was a teacher amongst teachers. She taught me how to do basically everything. She was my life!

I will attend my first meeting today. Jennifer will be here in an hour to pick me up. I'm really not sure what to expect, I mean, I don't have anything to offer anyone.

I do know that I wish Justin would call me. It's been weeks and I haven't heard from him. Isn't he concerned about knowing if I'm okay, not just me, but what about knowing if his own baby was okay?

Besides, he's the only person who's really cared about me since grandma. Everyone has their moments.

Even though everyone has stepped up their game with showing me love, I'm still not so sure of their motives or if their love is genuine. I guess in the long run we will see.

I head into the bathroom to put on my makeup on when the phone rings. It's Justin's mom. I'm shocked.

"Hello", I answer softly.

"Hi Faith, this is Justin's mom, are you busy"?

"No, I'm not busy at all", I answer her.

"Justin asked me to call you to see how you were doing".

"I'm doing okay, almost died though", I responded.

"Faith, I'm sorry to hear that. How's the baby?

"I lost the baby, when I passed out there wasn't enough oxygen, so the baby didn't make it", I said softly.

"I'm sorry to hear that, but you guys didn't need that baby anyway", she said in a devilish way.

"I'm sure you would think so", I responded.

"What makes you say that", she asked?

"Justin mentioned to me that you didn't like me nor want us to be together, because I don't have an upscale background. I know how people like you who are well-off look down on others who don't have much. However, it takes a person with integrity to lend a helping hand or words of care.

"Faith, I didn't say those things to hurt you, I simply was telling Justin, he can do better", she said abruptly.

"I'm going to end this conversation now", I said very respectfully.

"What about the warrant you have on my son", she asked?

"What about it? Everything he's done to me, and you ask me what about it. Obviously, you don't have any daughters or a heart, good bye Mrs. Romaine", I said as I ended the conversation.

The gullible nerve of her acting as if everything's my fault and not evaluating what her "momma's boy" did!

I'm so upset at this moment. I totally want to be left alone by everyone. I'm so burdened down right now and have many thoughts running through my mind.

All I want is for Justin to hold me in his arms. I want things the way they used to be when we first met.

I sat down on the bed and began to cry thinking of how I'm spinning out of control. I really need someone to talk to. This domestic violence group better do some justice for me, or else!

I can't take this madness, I really need to go somewhere and be alone. I feel like I'm at a turning point in my life.

The life obstacles I'm facing will either break me or make me. I'm determined to be made over!

What ever happened to the old Faith? The one who would brush it off and keep going?

Why am I so dependent on someone else's love and approval?

I'm a strong woman. With grandma not being here it will allow me to see just how strong I am and how much she's taught me.

Like how much I paid attention to her when she prayed and how she never gave up.

Yet, I allow myself to be broken, battered and bruised.

That's it, I decide to go to the group and get my help!

Jennifer arrives and we have another heart to heart conversation about Mrs. Romaine's nasty attitude.

"I'm still at awe she had the audacity and boldness to tell me in so many words Justin's not at fault", I said.

"Well, did she mention anything about Justin being wrong", Jennifer questions?

"Not a word, she didn't even apologize for her son's actions", I answered.

"That tells you a lot about where he came from and his background", Jennifer adds.

I thought about Jennifer's words.

"You know, Justin was brought up in a fine home, with his biological mom and dad; who gave him everything", I said.

"Just because they had good money, doesn't mean they have good teachings, morals and values", Jennifer replies.

"Yup, I guess you're right about that"!

"Besides, how much of Justin's background do you know", Jennifer asks.

Her words has me thinking. I think I'll give Amber a call later to see if she's heard anything about the situation, besides, I'm shocked she hasn't reached out to me. I wonder if anyone's told her about the incident.

"I'm really hoping to get something from the meeting", I tell Jennifer.

She assures me I would; I pray she's right.

On our way out my phone rings, it's Kevin. He's been hounding me lately, and being very protective.

I really do appreciate all the effort he's doing, but I don't want him to get the wrong idea.

My mind frame doesn't allow me to move past Justin. I can't stop thinking about what he's going through.

Kevin asks if he can cook dinner for me and the family tonight. I was very moved and touched, so I decided to let him.

Plus, who in the world would pass up a home cooked meal. My mom would be gracious to find she didn't have to cook dinner for me.

"That was nice of Kevin to ask me if he can come and cook for us", I mention to Jennifer.

"That's because he really likes you", Jennifer responded.

"You think so", I asked in a smart manner?

"Girl, please you're all he talks about. From the

beginning of my relationship with Darrin until now, Kevin's always talked about Ms. Faith", she said while laughing.

I began to laugh questioning Jennifer, "it's that serious"?

"Serious? Kevin told us that ever since high school he's had the biggest crush on you", Jennifer adds.

"Wow, I knew he liked me and we had our little moment the night of the prom, but I didn't think it was like that. Besides, we didn't do anything, but make out.

"Well whatever you offered him, he was very appreciative.

Besides, Kevin's a very nice guy, he has his head on straight and he knows where he's going in life", said Jennifer.

"He's a little too nice",
I said in a mocking way.
"What does that mean",
Jennifer asks?
"It means he's too nice,
some women want a man who's
a little jagged", I reply.
"You mean like Justin"?
I sat silently, thinking about
her question. Was she being
sarcastic or was her intention
meant for me to really think about
what I want from a man.
We reached the church by this
time, I look at the sign on the
front, it read "Domestic Violence
group this afternoon.
I looked at Jennifer.
"If I didn't know you any
better, I would think your
remark was a little cynical,
but you're the type to get a
person to thinking, and with
that in mind. Thank you", I
said in the most modest way

possible as I got out of her car.

The meeting lasted for an hour and a half. I was to meet Jennifer near the pastor's study when I was done. She was meeting Darrin at the church for their pre-marriage counseling.

They were still in the office meeting, so I head down a long hallway looking at all the art on the walls.

Then I reach a painting of a little old lady sitting in her rocking chair reading a book to small children.

The painting read, "Grandma's Teaching", the caption said …train up a child in the way which they should go and when they are older they will not depart far from it.

My thoughts began to go back to grandma's teachings and how she sat with me at night reading to me and telling me stories of when she were younger. Most importantly the many prayers we said together. I smiled to myself as I remembered those prayers.

"Hello young lady", an unfamiliar voice said coming from behind me.

I turned around to see a tall older man.

"Um, hello", I said giving a soft smile.

"Who are you", he asked.

"My name is Faith Ashby, I'm a friend of Jennifer and Darrin", I said.

"I'm Pastor Ben Johnson, Head Pastor of the church", he said.

"Very nice to meet you", I said as I handed my hand to shake the pastor's.

"I couldn't help seeing you smiling at this picture, does it mean something", he asked?

"Actually, it does, my grandma. She used to read and sing with me when I was younger", I explain.

"Yes, our parents and grandparents are very special influences in our lives", he said.

"Definitely", I agreed.

I look down the hall to see Jennifer and Darrin standing in the hall talking.

The pastor looks at me and says, "Your grandmother taught you well. Walk in the ways thereof."

I stood there astonished over the pastor's whispered words. He begins to walk away towards Jennifer and Darrin giving them a hug and handshake good-bye.

I turn and look at the painting again and walk off.

"So, you've met Faith", Jennifer said to Pastor Johnson.

"Yes, I did", he replied, turning to me, "hope to see you on Sunday, he said.

"Maybe".

It's four o'clock and I'm sitting waiting for Kevin to come over. He should be here around five, I think about what I'm going to say to Amber, since I haven't talked to her in a while.

I call her and she doesn't pick up. I don't leave a message. I'll just call her back. I look at the phone about to dial again, but the phone rings in my hands. It's Amber.

"Hey, how's everything going", Amber says.

"It's going", I answered.

"I just got back from Florida. I was there for three weeks visiting an old friend of mine. I miss you so much", Amber says.

"I miss you too", I answer.

"So what are you doing with yourself", Amber asks?

"You haven't heard what happened with me and Justin", I questioned?

"No, I haven't. Well, what happened, is everything okay", Amber asks?

I tell Amber the whole ordeal, and started crying. Then she did the most shocking thing ever···she apologizes.

"What are you apologizing for Amber, it's not your fault", I said to her.

"It is my fault, Faith, you don't understand. I knew what Justin was about. The old friend I went to visit in Florida is Justin's old girlfriend. I met her at a company event and we began talking, she started confiding in me and we became really good friends.

She told me the horrible things Justin was doing to her. I thought she was just exaggerating about his behavior. Until one day he came to work very upset. When I asked him what happened. He said that she had moved out while he was at work. He didn't know where she had gone.

I found out later she'd fled to her parent's house in Florida to get away from his abuse. Faith, I'm so sorry, it's my fault, because I didn't warn you, Amber said sobbing.

"Amber, why didn't you tell me, I don't understand. Do you know what I've been through", I yelled at her!

"I'm sorry Faith, years went by and you never said anything to me. I thought you two were happy, I thought everything was good in your relationship. You never told me anything about Justin's behavior, I thought he had changed. Please believe me Faith, I love you, I wouldn't want anything bad to happen to you", Amber said.

"I know, Amber, I know you love me like a sister. I kept it all to myself, because I didn't want anyone to know. I felt like it's our relationship and we just had to deal with our difficulties on our own. I don't know what I was thinking", I cried to Amber.

"Again, I'm sorry you went through all of the turmoil with him", said Amber.

Amber and I made arrangements to meet up for the weekend to talk and catch up. We agreed it's been way too long since we hung out. I tell her not to say a thing to Justin when she sees him at work.

She shocks me again by telling Justin had been fired from the job over six months ago. I couldn't believe my ears. I thought Justin was just having financial problems, not fired.

I guess Taylor was his job on the mornings he claimed he was heading to work. It all was coming out about Justin. What an idiot I was. I've been so dumb, I thought to myself.

After talking to Amber, I head up to the bathroom. I need a moment to adjust to all the news I had received.

I thought about Amber befriending Justin's ex-girlfriend and never even telling me. Why didn't she tell me? This is something which she didn't have to keep a secret.

Maybe she didn't tell me because she thought I would tell Justin everything she knew? Did she think she was protecting her? While in the long run I suffered.

As I thought about it, she's correct. I felt so connected to Justin, I would have told him.

The doorbell rang, it's probably Kevin. I really need a good friend to talk to.

I head to the door, look out the peep hole, but I don't see anyone.

I open the door and there's a package on the steps with my name on it. I look around, but don't see anyone. I pick up the package and take it in the house.

I look out the window and see Justin's car heading up the street. My heart is pounding.

I open up the package and it's a teddy bear, box of

chocolates and a note. The note read "I love you Faith; I'm sorry, please forgive me".

My heart drops.

I hid the package. If my mom or anyone saw it they would flip. I sat down on the couch and look down at my leg with the cast on it.

I read a message Kevin wrote on my cast and smiled. The message says "Don't give up pretty girl".

I felt my neck brace and the tears began to flow. I began to look back over my life and think about everything I've been through.

I'm only twenty-three years old and I feel broken-down.

With Justin showing up here makes me wonder.

The doorbell rings, my heart starts pounding again, it is Kevin this time.

He asks me how my day is going so far. I tell him, I'm taking it one day at a time.

He gets right down to cooking dinner, constantly looking at me from across the room. All I can do is smile at him. I never looked at him this way before.

"Why are you smiling so much", he asks.

"Nothing much, just never thought you could cook", I answer him.

"What? Girl you must don't know 'bout me! I'm really good", he says laughing.

"What are we having, and do you need any help", I asked?

"We're having Bar-B-Q chicken, baked mac-n-cheese and fresh kale greens and yes, you can help shred the cheese", he said smiling.

"Sure will".

Kevin comes over to me and takes my hands, puts them in a prayer position, places them up against his face and then he kisses them.

"What was that for", I asked?

"You're a very special young lady, who deserves the best", he answers me.

"Thanks, I needed that".

Mom and Michele pull up in the driveway. Kevin opens the door and grabs mom's bags. Mom tells us Lisa is doing great. Lisa took her first step today and is looking forward to coming home very soon.

I haven't seen my mom this happy in years. I was so happy for her.

As we sat around the table at dinner, something came to me. I was finally able to see that my family does love me.

My mom was blinded by the situations and problems her husband brought to her which didn't give her a chance to have happiness. I guess I can say the same about me. We all were all smiles, laughing and having a good time at dinner.

However, I was dying on the inside. I was wondering when my time will come. Not my time at having someone who loves me, but my time when I love myself.

"Well how are you feeling Faith today", mom asked.

"I'm feeling fine mom", thanks for asking.

"I'm glad you're okay", she said whole heartily.

"How was your session", asked Michele?

"It was interesting; I was able to hear so many stories which were similar to mine. I can't discuss them, but it was definitely an eye opener.

"Well, that's good, at least you know you're not by yourself", Michele said.

"Yeah, we're all here for you Faith", Kevin added.

"Thanks guys", I said with a sigh of relief.

7
I'm Woke

Last night was really nice. I really enjoyed myself with my family and Kevin, but of course that was overshadowed by my visitor and the gifts he left. Not to mention the information I received from Amber.

I have a lot to do today. Kevin will be taking me home to get more clothes and clean up a little bit. He's been a great help to me. He stops past my house every day to pick up the mail.

We're getting closer and I can feel the affection he has for me, but I'm not ready for anything right now. My main focus is starting school and getting a job. This leads me to my second errand today.

We're meeting Darrin to go over the business plans for his store. Plus, I will be filling out my application to get into school.

First things first, I have a group session this morning and Jennifer will be here soon.

I feel much better by staying busy. I don't want to sit around the house thinking about Justin.

I hear a car pull up. It must be Jennifer, but she's here early. I'm not even dressed. I look out the window, to my surprise I see Justin's car. Okay, this is getting creepy.

There's a knock at the door. I stand away from the window and stay quiet. I'm hoping he leaves. I don't want to talk to him. I have nothing to say.

For the first time in three years, I can see clearly about what I want out of life. Besides, how did he know I'm staying at my mother's house?

Could he be following me again? I try to glance out the window, but I don't see him or his car.

This time, I don't open the door. I don't want his presents.

My cell phone rings. It's Justin's mom. What does she want?

"Yes mam", I answered the phone as nicely as I could. I've never been the type to disrespect anyone's parents.

"Faith, how are you doing"?

"I'm doing fine", I say.

"Well, Justin has been trying to get in contact with you", she says.

"Why", I questioned.

"He wants to know why the police came to my house looking for him, didn't you talk to him about dropping the charges", she asks in a very vile manner.

"Well", answering her in the same manner, "had he not physically, verbally and mentally abused me, made me lose my baby, cheat on me, and push me down the stairs and left me for dead, the cops would not have come to your house to lock him up", I said.

"Faith, I never knew all of this was going on, please let's talk about it. Justin's just going through a tough time right now", she says.

"No, I'm going through a tough time right now".

"Faith please, everyone loses here", she said.

"Yes, everyone did lose, but I lost the most. I lost myself. I was so wrapped up in your son that I didn't care about me. I didn't care about what I needed and wanted in life. Now I know what I want and I know I can't love someone more than I love myself.

"So, how much is it going to cost for you to drop the charges", she asks cutting me off?

"I think the question is, how much your son's lawyer will cost, good bye", I said trying to end the conversation.

"Faith, you're making a big mistake, it's your words against his", she said.

"No, it's the police report with pictures, the doctor's reports with your son's DNA, a few witnesses and one desperate bitter victim. So tell your son it's best to just turn himself in", I added as I hung up the phone.

I had enough of this nonsense from her. She's very arrogant and believes she can intimidate me. Please, this isn't episodes of "mob moms and the sons who beat on women".

Anyway, I don't want anything to break my spirit today. So, let me start this day over.

I sat down on the bed, bowed my head and ⋯ I prayed.

I need God to bless me and do some great things in my life. The first thing I need is for him to help me out of this situation I'm in.

I didn't feel comfortable staying at my mom's house anymore. There's no telling what Justin is up to or planning. Therefore, I decided to go back home. I thought if I switch up my locations, I could confuse Justin.

I hear a car door close. I peep out the window. It's Jennifer. I tell her that I won't be coming back here for a few days, she asks why, but I don't respond.

I would just rather talk about something else other than me.

I ask her about the wedding plans. She asked me if I would be so gracious and be her maid of honor. Of course, I tell her I would be honored.

Jennifer looks at me acting as if she knows something's wrong. She asks me if everything's okay. Of course, I tell her.

Today's meeting was very good. I was able to share my story.

Today I learned the signs of domestic violence which consists of the feeling of being afraid of your partner, because you are afraid of angering that person.

You believe that you deserve to be hurt or mistreated for whatever reason.

In my case I believed that it was okay for Justin take his stress out on me because he was suffering. I believed it was okay, because we had been through so much together.

I felt as though he was the love of my life. Here, it's the total opposite. A person who loves you does not abuse you in any way.

How could I accept that? Love does not make you feel emotionally numb or helpless. He controlled who my friends were, put a GPS system on my car and continued with an unpredictable temper.

I never looked at it as being domestically abused. I thought that only happened to people who are older.

I never thought it could happen to me. He controlled how I would spin my money. He humiliated me in front of Taylor, and put me down.

I didn' t see his behavior as abuse, because it only happened a few times throughout our three year relationship. I thought it was a rough patch.

After the meeting, I went back to the hallway to take a picture of the painting which was on the wall…" Grandma' s Teachings" .

Then I head to the restroom. Once inside, I personally met one of the young ladies from the group, Marissa. She began telling me how much my story meant to her. She said she was going through the same thing with her husband.

I asked her what happened to him. She said the judge ordered him go to anger management and an alcohol abuse programs and she was ordered to domestic violence groups.

Hopefully, the judge knows what's best for all parties involved and hopefully this case will turn out for the best.

I was glad my story helped her. I see there is some good in coming to the group meetings. You find out, you're really not alone. You find there are many young women and men who are just like you; those who have the same situations and issues.

She asks me if I would be coming back this Sunday for church. I tell her I definitely would be coming back for Sunday services. I do believe God is giving me a second chance at life and a second, third and fourth chance to get things right.

Jennifer drops me off at Kevin's house for Darrin and me to go over the plans for his new project at his business.

"I want to bring you on as soon as you're finished healing", Darrin said in an amusing way, smiling at me.

"The sooner the better", I told him, giving him the eye, as if to say don't start with me.

He comes over and gives me the biggest hug.

"I love you so much, you're my little sister. We might not share the same mom and dad, but you're my family. I'm glad to have you back with me where I can look out for you", Darrin adds.

"I'm glad to be back with you guys, being able to talk, laugh and live", I tell him.

"I've missed you so much", Darrin said.

"I've missed you too, and I'm very sorry I allowed Justin to take me away from you all", I said with tears rolling down my face.

"It's going to be okay", Darrin assures me.

"Yup, it sure is"!

"So did you fill out your application for school", Darrin asks?

"Yes I did".

"I'm going to take her tomorrow for testing, Kevin adds.

"Great, so it's all coming together", said Darrin.

I tell them I am going to start school next semester and I wouldn' t care if I have one neck brace and two broken legs. Of course they found that to be very funny.

This is how it was when we were together. We all looked out for each other. Why I would ever allow myself to become apart from them I don' t know.

I didn' t find it necessary to tell them about Justin and his mom. I just want this to be over with so I can move on to the next chapter of my life.

Darrin leaves, leaving me alone with Kevin.

"So, are you up to going on a date with me", Kevin asks.

"A date? I guess I could accompany you on a date. However, I would not be caught dead at a restaurant with a neck brace and a cast on my leg; especially with writing on the cast as if I'm still in high school".

Kevin starts laughing, "Well, I guess I'm going to have to order in tonight", he said.

"Oh, so you want me to stay here with you for the evening", I ask?

"Sure, the guest bedroom is available for you".

"Good, cause I'm not ready for anything else", I tell him.

"I'm sure you're not, after all that you've gone through. Besides, I like your company and when you're ready, well if you're ready for a relationship, I hope I'm the guy for you".

"You're a really nice person, the type of person my mom approves of, my grandma would have approved of and most of all, the type I approve of. You've been taking really good care of me, thank you".

Then Kevin did the one thing I thought he wouldn't do at the moment. He lifted my leg, placed it on a pillow and took off my one shoe. I started laughing.

"What's so funny", he asks.

"Nothing, I thought you were going to make a move or something", I said.

"Nope, not until you're ready for me to make a move…do you want me to make my move now", Kevin asks joking?

"I think I'm going to do things the right way this time", I tell him trying to look innocent.

"Oh really"?

"Yes, I'm going to wait until I get married", I said.

From that statement, I just knew I would get a *"what in the world"* reply from Kevin.

"Well if that's what you want, I think you should do it. I know a lot of females who are practicing abstinence. It's an individual decision", he said.

"I think I'm going to do it until I'm mentally, physically and spiritually together, I said.

Kevin just smiled.

Last night was beautiful, Kevin and I stayed up talking about old times and catching up with each other.

I made a promise to the young lady in my group that I would come to church on Sunday. So, I decide to head home to get myself together.

I met Kevin downstairs. He was making breakfast. You're up early he said. I tell him I need to go home and get myself ready for church. To my surprise, he asks me if he could accompany me to church. Of course, I tell him!

I ask him if he could run me pass the hospital to see Lisa after church, he agreed.

He tells me my wishes are at his command. I just grinned, because he knows a man should be careful saying those words to a woman who loves making wishes!

On our way to church Kevin shared with me his goals of one day getting married. He asks me how I felt about having a family and kids.

I tell him family was really important to me and one day when I get myself on track, I would love to start a family.

He agreed and was glad I said those words. Kevin shared with me how much he would like for us to create our stepping stones together. I accepted.

We arrive at the church and met up with Darrin and Jennifer.

The church service starts. Pastor Johnson reads the scripture passage:

> Jude 1:3 *Beloved, although I was very eager to write to you about our common salvation, I found it necessary to write appealing to you to contend for the faith that was once for all delivered to the saints.*

The passage theme for his message was simply put ⋯. Contending for the Faith.

Wow, I thought, *Fighting for the Faith*. This message in my interpretation was for me, to fight for the faith I once had through my grandma's teaching. She delivered and taught me things which were needed to continue in life.

As I listen to the message, my mind took me to the things I need to fight for and have the faith that God would change them.

I decide to fight for faith with my relationship with my mom. Fight for faith in knowing Lisa will be healed completely. Fight for the faith in knowing everything will turn out alright in this situation with Justin. Fight for the faith in knowing

God is doing a new thing in my life. Fight for the faith in knowing that with God all things are possible. Most importantly, fight for the faith, which means fight for me!

I sat there captivated, while Pastor Johnson spoke and I became instantly inspired and motivated by his words.

I thought about the painting, the way I was living my life and how I was mentally struggling with understanding what love really means. Grandma used to repeat I Corinthians 13:4-13, *Love is patient, love is kind. It does not envy, it does not boast, it is not proud. It does not dishonor others, it is not self-seeking, it is not easily angered, love keeps no record of wrong doings. Love does not delight in evil, but rejoices with the truth. It always protects, always trusts, and always hopes, always perseveres.* That scripture teaches what love is and should be. I had finally come to realize that Justin does not love me, because if he did, he would not hurt me, physically, mentally, or spiritually. I had made up my mind to finally let go and let God.

After church, I saw Marisa, the young lady from my group. She came over and gave me a big hug. I tell her how I loved the message on this morning.

She asks me if I were coming back. I tell her I would definitely be back next Sunday.

I know now that God was speaking to me threw his Word and my grandma. It's time for me to change my lifestyle. I decided it was time for me to get focused and motivated in serving God. After service, we visit Lisa and then Kevin drops me off at home.

Kevin dropped me off after seeing Lisa. We were happy to see she's coming along just fine.

Could this day get any better?

When I arrive home I had an envelope with my name on it. I open it and it was from Justin.

I should tear it up, but something inside me wants to read it. I open it.

Faith, I love you, can I please talk to you, the letter read. Just then, the phone rings, it's Justin. Can we talk he asks. He tells me again, how sorry he was.

Wow, I'm thinking to myself, where have I heard this before. I listen and the sound of his voice doesn't seem to mesmerize me anymore.

Actually, it makes me mad. I'm mad that I allowed you to get into my mind, body and soul I finally answer.

Please leave me alone. I need to heal I tell him. He starts yelling in the phone.

"Listen you're just as worthless as my mom said you are. You were nothing when I met you and your nothing now. Do you think I'm going to allow you to destroy my life"?

"I can't believe you think I'm responsible for your actions. You hurt me, you killed our baby. It was you"!

"So, you're not going to drop the charges", he asked?

I could hear noise outside my back door. I hop over to the back window and see Justin standing outside, but he doesn't see me, because his back is turned to me.

I get on my house phone and dial 911. I couldn't say anything, so I just let the operator hear me talking to Justin.

"I'll think about dropping the charges", I tell him in fear".

"You're a lair" Justin yelled!

Just then, I heard the door break. Justin runs towards me grabbing me. He throws me across the room. I fall, since I can't catch my balance with this cast. Then again, when have I ever been able to catch my balance when it comes to Justin?

I stand up as quickly as I could as Justin comes over to me. He punches me in the face, grabs me, rips off my neck brace, and puts his hands around my neck. He began to squeeze.

I can't breathe. With one hand I try to pry his hands off my neck, with the other I try to reach for my clog, I notice on the floor. If I'm going to die this time, it won't be without the fight of my life.

I grab the clog; take it upside Justin's head, once, twice, three times. He lets my neck go and falls on the floor holding his head. I take my fist and with all of my might punching him in the face, one blow, two, and three. He's bleeding from his mouth and head.

I get up and try to run, I mean hop out the door. He comes behind me grabs me by the hair and toss me across the room. I hit my back on the lower part of the wall

Then he takes out a knife and walks towards me. The doorbell rings.

"Police", screams one of the officers from outside.

"I'm in here. Help me", I scream!

The police kicks the front door down after hearing my plea. Justin drops the knife and runs towards the back door, but the officer grabs him and throws him up against the wall.

I watch as they give him a couple more blows. Then one of the officers rushes to my aid.

They call the ambulance for me. This is my second time in three months, back to the hospital I go.

As I sat in the ambulance, I began to think. Was the love Justin and I had real? Was it worth my life, my time, my very being? Why was I so attached to him and why didn't I see him for who he really is?

I believed his every word; I believed that nothing and no one could come between us. We belonged together; he was my all and all.

My mind began to play back the church message, Contending for the

Faith. I thought about my fight and I thought about my life. I cannot believe the amount of faith I had in Justin.

As the tears flowed down my face; I had to come to a realization that I needed to get my relationship back with God. God is a jealous God and no relationship will work if I did not put Him first.

My mind went back to one of Grandma's teachings when she would sit me down on Tuesdays and go over some of the Bible stories.

I thought about the story of the creation, how God told man he could eat anything in the Garden, but not to eat the forbidden fruit. Grandma made it clear, that even in life, God forbids us to have certain things in our lives, because they cause us harm. For our protection, we must obey.

That goes for relationships and friendships as well. It was time for me to wise up and began listening to what God was saying, and not what my heart was saying. In reality, no one wants the feeling of loneliness. I had finally realized I wasn't alone.

I thought back to the domestic violence group. I'd learned how to recognize domestic violence for the ugly face it was. Violent or aggressive behavior is more than emotional abuse, it's a pattern of abusive behavior. It's when someone tries to gain or maintain control over another.

I was allowing myself to let the psychological actions and threats of Justin go. He was no longer going to have power over me!

I'm back at the hospital my family and friends were once again here to support me.

I sit there glancing at them, this throws them off. I guess they're probably wondering if I'm crazy or bumped my head way too many times.

"What are you thinking about girl", Darrin asks?

"Yes, after what you just been through; and the fight you have ahead of you, yet you sit there as if everything is okay", Michele asks?

"Yes, everything is okay, even when I'm faced with adversity, because I know it won't last long.

No more will I allow anything or anyone to place me into a position, I don't want to be in. Right now, I'm looking forward to Lisa coming home. I'm happy I have my mom and sisters with me. I have my close friends. I'm looking forward to working and going to school. Yes, I know everything will be alright because I realize that I'm-- I'm free".

The doctor discharges me and tells me how lucky I am, once again, that it's nothing serious. Just a few bumps and bruises, but I'll be fine.

Well, we're heading home and the ride seems much shorter this time. Maybe because, I realize I have to go back to the same house where it all took place.

Something within me had to realize that in that same house once lived one of the most upstanding women I knew. My Grandma Peggy was a woman with morals, values, work ethic, and class. She had taught me everything she knew and one of the most important things that she taught me was the power of prayer.

I remember her telling me that prayer changes things.

I sat back and within my heart, I started to pray. I asked God if He would give me the strength to move forward and to replace Justin with Jesus.

I knew that God couldn't take away the memories, but he could take away the ill feelings I now carry for Justin. I can't forget, but I can forgive and with forgiveness comes the forgetfulness of my pain.

I didn't want to remember the pain; I wanted to remember how I overcame.

I can't wait to get back to church to tell the ladies how I overcame this attack. I knew it would be a big help for someone else who's going through a similar abuse as I am.

After everything that Justin has put me through, I thought my biggest pleasure would be facing him in court, but it's not.

I wonder if losing his job, and not having the mental stability contributed to his rage. I began to look at how things took a turn for the worse. We started our relationship based on love, but then it became control. I allowed Justin to take control of me, because I thought he loved me.

Prayerfully, Justin will find a different way of handling his problems in life besides taking it out in rage.

He has to realize that the end result to our problems in life should not end with hostility, aggression and hurting others. I pray he fights for the faith in his life.

As we were on our way home, I sat in the back of the car. I thought about the time I was lying on the ground lifeless, grandma asked me the question, *"Faith what are you doing"* ?

"Grandma", I whispered, as I lifted my head towards Heaven, *"I'm Fighting for the Faith"*.

Acknowledgements

I would like to acknowledge and extend my heartfelt gratitude to my family and friends. Words alone cannot express what I owe them for their encouragement and whose patient love has enabled me to complete this book.

A special thanks to Pastor, Elder Leighton McMillian and his wife, Evangelist Deborah McMillian of Emmanuel, Church of God In Christ, York, PA for giving me the idea for the name of the book and the scripture Luke 1:3. To my photographer Zuri Frazier and Illustrator Kia Street for going the extra mile with the kind of feedback that put pen to paper again and again.

And especially to God, who made all things possible.